The Extraordinarily Ordinary Life of Cassandra Jones

Episode 2: Club Girls

The Extraordinarily Ordinary Life of Cassandra Jones
Walker Wildcats Year 1
Episode 2: Club Girls
Tamara Hart Heiner

Print edition
copyright 2015 Tamara Hart Heiner
cover art by Octagon Lab
Illustrations by Elisa Allan

Also by Tamara Hart Heiner:
Perilous (WiDo Publishing 2010)
Altercation (WiDo Publishing 2012)
Deliverer (Tamark Books 2014)

Inevitable (Tamark Books 2013)
Lay Me Down (Tamark Books 2016)

Tornado Warning (Dancing Lemur Press 2014)

TABLE OF CONTENTS

Episode 2: Club Girls

CHAPTER ONE

Ice Cream Treat

Monday.

Cassie ignored the butterflies in her stomach as she entered her fifth-grade classroom. The weekend had been rather emotional. For the first time since moving to Arkansas, she'd spent the night at a friend's house. But because of the stupid fight over a dog, Cassie wasn't sure if they were still friends.

She waited in the bathroom during break and cornered Riley as soon as she came out of the stall.

Riley hesitated, something like fear flashing across her face before her green eyes hardened. "What do you want?" She lifted her chin, the short strawberry-blond hair just grazing her neck.

"I wanted to apologize," Cassie said. "I was rude to you at your house on Saturday. And I had a nice time before that." Before Riley hid the dog from Cassie, anyway. "I want to be friends again."

Riley hesitated, and then the stiffness left her shoulders. "Why?"

"Well. . . ." Cassie hadn't really expected that question, and she blurted out the truth. "Because they called your name at church, and we're supposed to be friends!" She followed Riley to the sink and squirted soap on her hands.

"They said my name at your church?" Riley squinted at her over the water, both of them washing their hands. "But I don't go to church."

"I know." Cassie nodded. A few strands of her straight brown hair had escaped her pony tail, and they floated around her face. She slicked them back. "But you're supposed to. This is why we're—" Cassie hesitated to use the term, but she did. She crossed her fingers that Danelle, her first friend in Arkansas, wouldn't hear. "Best friends."

Riley lowered her eyes, but not before Cassie saw her smile. She smiled too, glad that they weren't fighting anymore.

Cassandra had just moved to Arkansas from Texas this year, and the first few weeks of school had been confusing, both mentally and emotionally, as she tried to figure out her role and make new friends. She considered herself lucky now; she had two best friends, Danelle Pierce and Riley Isabel. The two girls didn't like each other, but Cassie figured as long as she kept them apart, that didn't matter.

"I'll ask my mom about why they mentioned me at your church," Riley said as they exited the bathroom and got back in line in the hallway. "She'll know."

The class continued down the hall for P.E. Cassie partnered up with Danelle for catch.

"What's going on with you and Riley?" Danelle asked, the metal from her braces reflecting the overhead lights in the cafeteria. "You're like, all buddies now."

Cassie didn't know if she should feel guilty about having two best friends, but she did. "I spent the night at her house on Friday. We're really good friends now."

"You've never come to my house," Danelle said, tossing her the ball.

Danelle had never invited. "I'd love to come. Or you come to my house," she said instead. She tossed the ball back.

"I saw you reading *The Babysitters Club*. Do you like

those books?"

"Love them!" Cassie said, brightening. She loved to read more than anything else in the world. "Do you like them?"

"Yeah, I've read a few of them. They're fun."

"We should start our own club!" Cassie gasped, catching the ball again. She and her sister Emily had already talked about doing that, but just the two of them could hardly make up a club. "You, me, Riley—"

"Riley?" Danelle interrupted, wrinkling her nose.

Cassie didn't want to leave Riley out. "Well, three people isn't very many."

Danelle hesitated. "I guess we could try it. I don't know, though. She's so annoying."

Cassie was too excited about Danelle agreeing to worry about her jibe toward Riley. "I can't wait! It's going to be so much fun!" She envisioned them sitting around her room with the telephone, waiting for

5

people to call them and schedule babysitting assignments, just like they did in the books. She tossed the ball again to Danelle, who laughed.

"I'll tell my mom. Call me and we'll plan when to come over."

♥

Cassie waited until Ms. Dawson had finished giving them a workbook assignment and the class was too occupied to notice her. Everyone had their books open, pencils scribbling, when she stealthily removed her reading book from her desk. She opened it up just to be sure. All twenty squares had a sticker in them, proof that she had read twenty new books since the beginning of the school year. The reward was an ice-cream trip with her fifth-grade teacher.

She pushed back her chair and tiptoed to the desk, the book tucked under her arm. "Here," she whispered, dropping it in front of Ms. Dawson. She started back to her seat when Ms. Dawson said, "Come here, Cassie."

Cassie turned around as Ms. Dawson opened the book. She raised one eyebrow. "You've already read this many books?"

Cassie nodded. "I love to read."

Ms. Dawson looked at her, one eye squinting slightly. "Can you make a list of all the books you read?"

"Um, sure." She hoped she could remember them, anyway. She sat down, her heart pounding with the added pressure. She knew she should start on her workbook assignment, but she needed to write down these book titles before she forgot!

It took some thought, but most of the titles came easily enough. She'd read several from the same series, and that wasn't too hard to remember. But she got to number eighteen and couldn't think of the last three books. She took the sheet back to Ms. Dawson, blinking hard so she wouldn't cry.

"I can't remember the last three. I'll have to go home and look through my books."

Her teacher tilted her head and read through the list. "That's all right, Cassie. This is good enough." She looked up and smiled. "I'll call your mom today and set up a time to take you out for ice-cream."

Cassie beamed back at her. "Okay!" She skipped back to her chair and finally got started on the assignment.

♥

"So your teacher called me today," Mrs. Jones said as Cassie unloaded the dishwasher. "She said she wants to take you out for ice-cream."

"Oh, yeah!" Cassie turned around. "It's okay, right? It's because I already read twenty books."

"Of course it's fine. I think it's great that your teacher is so involved."

"Yeah, she's awesome." Cassie turned back to the dishes, thinking of something else. "Can we start a babysitters club?"

"A what?"

"I'll show you." She put the last cup in the cupboard, then ran out of the room to get one of her books. In the back was a flier that said, "Start your own babysitters club!" It listed the steps needed to get something like that going, followed by testimonials from other girls who had successfully started their own clubs.

Her mom took it from her hand and read over it. "Do I need to pay for anything?"

Cassie shook her head. "No. We'll spread the word and meet here once a week, and people will call us to babysit."

"Well, I guess that's okay. Who do you want in your club? Are you including your sister?"

"Yes."

"Sure. You can start it."

Cassie squealed and threw her arms around her mom's neck. "Thanks so much!"

♥

Cassie gathered Danelle and Riley at recess the next day.

"I got permission to start the babysitters club," she said, squeezing their fingers excitedly. "My mom said you can come over on Thursday night and we can get started. Does that sound good?"

"Yeah," Danelle said, nodding. "I'm in."

"I'll ask my mom," Riley said. "But I think I can do it.

Cassie looked at her two friends, Riley with short strawberry-blond hair, Danelle with shoulder-length brown hair and braces. She had so much hope that they'd become great friends, also.

♥

"You can sit up here with me." Ms. Dawson opened

the passenger door to her long, silver car and gestured for Cassie to get in.

Cassie did, though she felt very awkward climbing into her teacher's car. She folded her hands together in her lap and sat up straight.

Ms. Dawson started the car. "I'm very impressed that you read all those books so quickly. You must really like to read."

Cassie nodded. She relaxed a little bit in her seat. "Yeah. It's my favorite thing to do."

"Have you ever tried writing?"

"Writing?" She'd never really thought about it. It sounded so boring. But then she remembered the two stories she'd started in fourth grade. "I started some silly stories last year, but I haven't really written since then." Silly stories, all right. One about an evil monster who became friendly, and another about four orphans who had to move in with their aunt. Neither story got past the third chapter.

"It's been my observation that people who like to read also like to write."

Cassie didn't like writing down notes in class, and she hated copying things off the blackboard. *I might be the one reader who proves that wrong*, she thought.

They pulled up to the ice-cream shop, and she followed Ms. Dawson inside.

"What would you like?" Ms. Dawson asked.

It just seemed wrong to tell her teacher to buy something for her. Cassie surveyed the menu behind the counter. "Could I have a vanilla waffle cone, please?"

She sat down at a booth and waited while Ms. Dawson placed the order. What would they talk about? Tomorrow's assignment? Her grades? This just seemed so weird.

"So," Ms. Dawson said, returning with the ice cream,

"what do you think of Arkansas so far?"

If she had asked Cassie a few weeks ago, the answer would've been very different. "I like it, I think. It's different than Texas. But I'm making friends. I like the school." And now that they were moved into their new house, everything felt better. "We have a dog and a cat. I want another dog, but my mom won't let me have one."

"One dog can be enough."

Cassie shrugged. "Yeah." Riley had a dog that Cassie just loved, and Riley's family was willing to give it to the Joneses. But Cassie's mom put her foot down on the idea.

They chatted about Cassie's family and the new house, and then Cassie's ice-cream was gone. They got back in the car and Ms. Dawson turned to Cassie.

"Where do you live, Cassandra?"

Cassie squinted at the road, not even sure where she

was. She tried to visualize the turns her mom made when she picked her up from school once a week. Not that it did much good, because they weren't even at the school. "Go left," she said, because she was pretty sure left was the correct direction.

Ms. Dawson pulled out onto the main road. Seven minutes went by before she ventured, "Am I supposed to turn anywhere, Cassie?"

There were farther out of the city now, with empty pastures and fields dotting the road beside out-buildings and antique shops. "I'm not sure," Cassie admitted. "This looks familiar. We turn left somewhere in here, but I'm not sure where."

Ms. Dawson gave her a look that Cassie couldn't identify. Exasperation? Frustration? Annoyance? She sank into her seat, willing herself invisible. Great. She'd just managed to ruin things with her teacher.

Ms. Dawson pulled the car over into a gas station.

She fished around in her purse until she found a cell phone. "I'll call your mom and get directions."

Cassie nodded but didn't say a word. She figured the less she talked, the less Ms. Dawson would remember being upset with her.

"Hi, Karen, this is Ms. Dawson, Cassandra's teacher. Yes, I'm fine, how are you? Listen, we have a small problem here. No, no, nothing urgent." She laughed. "I'm bringing her home, and she can't remember how to get there."

Cassie squeezed her eyes shut, her face burning with humiliation.

"We're at a gas station right off the highway. Oh, okay. Uh-huh. Sure, I got it. We'll see you soon." She put the phone away and slid the car out of the gas station. "It's all right, Cassandra. We're on the right road, we just didn't go far enough."

Cassie uttered a sigh of relief. At least she hadn't led

them miles off course or into a different city.

Ms. Dawson made a left turn at the next signal, and everything began to look more familiar. The curvy, two-lane road, the trees hovering over the tops of it, the cows and ponds.

"Oh, this looks right," Cassie said.

"Yes, your mom thought you'd start to recognize it as we got closer." She slowed down on some of the tighter curves. They came around a corner, and Cassie pointed to the statue of a big white bull standing guard at the top of a gate.

"That's the white bull." It was what her mom always told her to look for because it meant she was going the right way.

Ms. Dawson didn't comment. Several minutes later, she made the final turn up the gravel road that led to Cassie's house. She slowed down around the potholes, the car churning and fuming as it climbed the steep hill. "No one could expect you to remember how to get here, Cassie."

She'd never called her by her nickname before. Her teacher wasn't mad at her. She didn't think Cassie was ridiculous for not knowing the way home. Cassie's shoulders relaxed.

Ms. Dawson pulled into the circle drive in front of Cassie's home. Their new house. They'd only moved in a few weekends ago.

"This is a lovely home, Cassandra," Ms. Dawson said, getting out of the car.

"Thank you." She grabbed her backpack and slid out also. She spotted her mother coming down the porch steps. "And thanks for the ice-cream."

"It's a pleasure to have you in my class, Cassie."

Her chest warmed under the praise. She nodded and hurried into the house, leaving her mother to talk to Ms. Dawson.

CHAPTER TWO

Smart Kids

"Are you doing Odyssey of the Mind?" Emmett Schrimmer asked Cassie during math. He and Matthew Grace sat closest to her.

"I don't know what that is," Cassie replied, penciling in her answer on her paper. It didn't look right, so she erased it and tried again.

"It's this really hard contest for smart kids. You have to build things and answer creative questions."

Matthew rolled his eyes. "It's not for smart kids. It's for anyone who's interested."

"Yeah, but only the smart kids are interested," Emmett returned.

"Why are you asking?" Cassie asked, interrupting their argument.

"Well, we form teams," Emmett said. "And we need one more person on our team. You could do it." He lowered his voice. "The coolest part is, we get to leave class twice a week to practice."

That was a very appealing thought. "Okay. I'll do it."

"Great!" Emmett said. "My mom's the coach. I'll tell her you joined."

The next day Cassie took home paperwork for her mom to sign. "I need you to sign this," she said. "Or I can't join the Odyssey of the Mind team."

"What's that?" her mom asked.

"A team for smart kids. And we get to leave class to

practice."

Mrs. Jones frowned. "I've never heard of it. I'll take a look at this."

Cassie hovered close by, waiting for the coveted signature.

"Don't you have chores to do, young lady?" her mother said, shooing her off. Cassie sighed and went to unload the dishwasher.

She finished, and her mom still hadn't supplied her with the paperwork. Cassie went back to her mom's room. "Well? Did you sign it?"

Mrs. Jones put down the book she was reading and straightened her glasses. "It's a lot of practices and a huge time commitment. Not just in school, Cassandra, but after school too. And if you commit, I commit. Are you sure you're going to do it?"

Cassie nodded, quite certain this was what she wanted. "Yeah. It'll be fun."

"All right." Her mom sighed like it physically hurt her, but she signed her name on the dotted line. "Here you go."

❤

Cassie joined Emmett and a handful of other kids as they were let out of class after lunch. "So what do we do at practice?"

"Well, first we have to see if you like it."

"If I like it?" Cassie frowned. "What's there not to like?"

"Maybe you won't think it's fun? I don't know. And you have to feel comfortable with your teammates. You'll be working on challenges with them."

"I thought I was on your team."

"Well, kind of." He raised his eyebrows at her. "It depends on where you're needed, also. We always have a challenge practice, and we're scored on our participation."

"What challenges?" Cassie could feel the beginnings of panic building in her chest. No one had said anything about performing in front of anyone. "Will I be doing that today?"

"Yeah. Don't worry. We all do it. It's easy."

She was definitely panicking now. Cassie's breathing came in fast and hard, and she curled and uncurled her fingers, trying to get life back into them. "I changed my mind. I don't want do to this."

They came to a stop outside another classroom door, this one set up very differently than the others. It had four tables inside and one podium in front.

"You'll be fine," Emmett said again. He slipped past her into the room.

Cassie wanted to turn and run back to class. Instead she came in with the rest of the students. She hoped no one could see the way her knees wobbled.

"Hi, I'm Mrs. Holland," a woman standing by the

door said. "I'm the teacher in charge of special events here at Walker. You must be Cassandra Jones?" She consulted a piece of paper in front of her, one with Cassie's mom's signature spread across the bottom. "We're excited to have you. Sit at a table, please."

Cassie nodded and turned around. The other students had all sat down, four to a table. That left only one with a spot. The one at the very end. Cassie recognized Janice from Girls' Club and sat by her.

"Hi, Cassie," Janice said, scooting her chair over to make room.

"Wait, she's on our team?" a boy that Cassie didn't recognize said.

"These aren't your official teams," Mrs. Holland said, standing at the podium at the front. "We'll organize teams later. Right now we're just going to run through some drills. This is the trivia part. Team A, you'll start. You can discuss the answer as a team, but only the team captain answers. Decide quickly who your team captain is going to be."

The other kids all seemed to know each other, so Cassie stayed quiet as her team (Team D) argued and decided on Jerry Freeman, the boy she didn't know, as the captain.

"Question one. What food makes up nearly all of a Giant Panda's diet?"

Team A leaned toward each other and deliberated back and forth before Emmett stood up. "The bamboo."

"That is correct." Mrs. Holland made a tally mark on the board. "Team B. True or false? Mice live for up to ten years."

Were all of these questions about animals? Cassie could only hope she'd get a true or false one. She straightened up as it neared her team's turn, her heart hammering so hard in her chest she thought she'd throw up.

"Team D. What is the name of the phobia that involves an abnormal fear of spiders?"

Her team huddled up. "It's a phobia," Jerry whispered. "So it probably has the word phobia in it."

Janice nodded. "Like claustrophobia."

"So something phobia," the other boy, Kayne, said. "What's another word for spider?"

"Insect?" Jerry suggested.

Janice shook her head. "Spiders aren't insects. They have eight legs, not six."

"Time's almost up," Mrs. Holland said.

Cassie held very still, hoping no one would remember her if she didn't move.

"If they're not insects, they're arachnids," Kayne said.

"Arachnid phobia?" Janice said.

Jerry snapped his fingers. He stood up and said, "Arachnophobia."

"That's correct." Mrs. Holland gave their team a tally mark.

"How did you know that?" Janice asked.

"I saw a movie once with that name, all about crazy spiders." He grinned, obviously pleased with himself.

They fell silent as the other teams went through their questions. Cassie tried to guess the answers before the team captains shouted them out, but she didn't know them. Not any of them.

"Team D," Mrs. Holland said, turning to them again. "What is the largest type of big cat in the world?"

Big cat. Cassie listed them in her head. Tiger, cheetah, panther, lion, cougar. But she couldn't begin to guess which was the largest.

"Lions are huge," Jerry was saying. "They can weigh like five hundred pounds."

"So is that our answer?" Janice asked.

"Are we sure they're the biggest?" Kayne asked.

Jerry turned to Cassie. "Don't you have any guesses?"

There it was, the direct question. Cassie's face burned. "I don't know. Maybe a panther?"

Jerry rolled his eyes. "A panther isn't a type of cat. It's another word for big cats like leopards and jaguars."

"Oh." She shrugged. "The jaguar, then."

"Time!" Mrs. Holland said.

Jerry stood up and faced the front. "The lion."

Mrs. Holland shook her head. "Sorry, that's incorrect. The correct answer is, the tiger."

Jerry glared at them all as he sat down. "Thanks a lot."

"None of us knew, Jerry," Janice said, pushing her short brown hair behind her ear.

"Yeah, well, some of us know nothing at all." His gaze fell on Cassie.

She turned away, humiliation warming her neck and

face. She didn't want to do this anymore. At least her mom would be relieved not to have to drive her to all the practices.

"This next part is a problem for all of you to work out as a team. Take ten minutes," Mrs. Holland said, going to the board. She wrote several sentences and then stepped to the side.

Cassie squinted at the board, but Mrs. Holland's

handwriting was slanted and tiny. She couldn't make out the words.

"What species should we use?" Janice asked.

"Something with a small name," Jerry said. "Like cat or dog."

"But that's too easy," Kayne said. "It would be more creative to do a longer name. Like chinchilla or guinea pig."

"I like chinchilla," Jerry snorted. "The chinchilla eats a quesadilla."

Janice laughed, her shoulders shaking. "You so don't pronounce the l's in quesadilla."

"So? It rhymes." He looked at Cassie. "You just don't have any opinions about anything, do you?"

"I don't know what we're doing," Cassie admitted.

"Wow, shockers," Jerry said. "You can't read, either? What are you even doing here?" He looked around the room toward Emmett's table. "I'm gonna have to talk to

Emmett about who he invites here."

Cassie blinked, close to tears by his harsh words. "I can't see the board."

"Right," he snorted.

Janice shot him a glare and swiveled in her chair to face Cassie. "We're making rhymes with animals. We decide which animal and make a rhyme, like, 'the cat is wearing the hat.' Got it?"

Cassie nodded, but she wasn't really listening. She didn't care anymore. She stood up. "I have to use the bathroom." She walked over to Mrs. Holland, ignoring the way Jerry and Kayne leaned together and started whispering. "Mrs. Holland? Can I go to the bathroom?"

"Sure," Mrs. Holland said. "We only have about five minutes left. You can just go back to class when you're done."

Cassie exhaled in relief. "Okay."

"How were things today? Did you get the hang of it?"

Cassie faked a huge smile. "Sure. It was fun."

"Perfect. Will we see you next week?"

"Um, I don't know," Cassie said, shifting her weight from one foot to the other. "My mom said it might be hard to work into her schedule."

"But it's during the school day."

"I know. I mean, all the other practices. I'll let Emmett know." Cassie gave a brief wave and fled the room before Mrs. Holland could ask any more questions.

She bypassed the bathroom entirely. She didn't really need to go. She just had to get out of that room that made her feel *claustrophobic*, away from those arrogant people who made spiders seem friendly.

CHAPTER THREE

Glasses

"Today we'll have an eye screening," Ms. Dawson said on Friday. She finished writing their spelling words on the board. "After you've written your sentences, line up at the door."

Eye screenings were nothing new. Cassie remembered doing them every year at her old school. "Look at the apple," they always said. But she never needed glasses.

She glanced around at her classmates, noting those who had glasses and those who didn't. Glasses were like one more piece of jewelry. And they made people look smarter. Both of her parents had glasses, so it was just a matter of time before she needed them too. Or so she hoped.

The kids trooped down the hall to another room where several computers were set up. Cassie waited in line patiently until it was her turn.

"What's your name?" the parent volunteer asked.

"Cassandra Jones."

The woman wrote that down on her sheet of paper, other students' names cascading down in a row. "Ms. Dawson's class?"

"Yes."

"Okay." She put the pen down and repositioned the machine, lowering it down to Cassie's height. "Put your chin right here and press your forehead into the

33

top bar."

Cassie did as instructed.

"Can you see the red apple on the picnic table?"

She saw it with perfect clarity. "Yes."

"How about now?"

She squinted, but it was still clear. "Yes."

"Okay." The image changed to rows of letters. "Can you read me the letters on the second line?"

"E A F G P." The last letter was B, but Cassie pretended like she couldn't see it.

"And the third line?"

These were blurry, but Cassie could read them. G B C D E. "O P C D B."

"And the fourth line."

A F E B G. "I can't read them."

"All right, thank you, Cassandra."

Cassie dutifully backed away from the machine, letting someone else take her place. She squeezed her fingers together. It probably wouldn't mean anything. She probably hadn't done bad enough to need glasses. She pushed the thought from her head and decided not to wonder about it for now.

Easier said than done. Cassie kept thinking about the screening over the next few days, wondering when she'd know, if she'd know.

She didn't have to wait too long. A few days later, the intercom buzzed.

"Ms. Dawson?"

Ms. Dawson stopped in the middle of her lecture. "Yes?"

"Can you send Ciera Lamb, Emmett Schrimmer, Maureen Hemming, and Cassandra Jones to room two-thirteen, please?"

"Yes, Ma'am." Ms. Dawson nodded at the four students.

Cassie jumped up and joined them, eager to get out

of the classroom and find out why they were needed. She knew the two girls well from Girls' Club, and Emmett had continued to be friendly even after she dropped out of Odyssey of the Mind. "What do you think it is?" she asked as they walked through the halls. She thought of the eye screening. It was all she had thought about for days.

"I don't know," Emmett said.

"Maybe we failed our eye exam," Cassie said, pressing the issue.

"I hope not!" Maureen said, her blue eyes going wide. "I don't want glasses!"

"I would love them." Cassie's hand dropped to the beaded necklace she wore, fingering the large plastic baubles. "I think it would be so fun."

Sure enough, they walked into the classroom and saw the same machines set up as last time. Cassie's heart rate sped up. Should she lie again? She couldn't even remember what she'd said on the first one. What if she got it wrong?

It went much faster this time. Their names were already on a list, and a man called them out one by one. When it was Cassie's turn, she sat at the machine as instructed. He skipped the apple part and went straight to the lines.

"Can you read the first line?" he asked.

That one was easy. "Yes," Cassie said, and recited the letters.

"The second line?"

She could. She licked her lips. She opted for just mixing up the letters.

"And the third line?"

She shook her head. "It's blurry." Which was true, but she could still see everything.

"All right, thank you, Cassandra. You can go back to class."

She was the last one, but her classmates had waited for her.

"You were right," Ciera said. "It was about the eye exams."

"I sure hope I passed this time," Maureen said.

Cassie was pretty sure she hadn't passed.

❤

"Cassie." Ms. Dawson came to her desk right before school ended and handed her a slip of paper. "Put this in your backpack and give it to your mom, please."

It was folded in half so Cassie couldn't see the words, but she was dying open it. "Okay." She'd take it out on the bus and read it.

She sat down by Betsy Lemo. Betsy was in a different class, but since they rode the same bus, they were friends.

"What's that?" Betsy asked as Cassie retrieved the piece of paper from her backpack.

"A note from my teacher."

"Oo, you in trouble?"

"Of course not," Cassie scoffed. She unfolded the note.

"And you're going to read it?" Betsy gasped. She leaned in closer.

Cassie pulled it away, holding it above her head. "You can't read it! I have to know what it says before I give it to my mom."

Betsy rolled her eyes. "That's kind of like cheating."

Cassie ignored her and read over the note.

Mrs. Jones,

Cassandra failed her second eye screening this morning. Please make an appointment with the optometrist of your choice to verify if she needs to use corrective lenses.

"Yes!" Cassie exclaimed, pumping her fists in the air.

"What, it's something good?" Betsy said.

"I need glasses." Cassie couldn't stop grinning.

"And that's good news?"

"Yeah!" Cassie shook her head. "I've been wanting them for years! I'm so excited!"

Her mom wasn't quite as excited. She made an appointment for the following day, and as they drove to the doctor, she said, "Glasses are expensive, Cassie. You can't change your mind or quit wearing them just because you don't want to anymore."

"I'll love them!" Cassie exclaimed, offended her mother would even think she might not.

Her mom grumbled under her breath and didn't say anything more.

The doctor was quite thorough, asking Cassie all kinds of questions before even pulling up the letter chart. He made her a bit nervous. Somehow she felt he'd know if she lied about what she could see.

Finally he sat her down in the chair and had her recite the letter lines.

Cassie squinted a little bit and took her time, pausing on some letters as if they were hard to make out.

"Thank you, Cassie," he said when she finished. He jotted down a few notes and turned to her mother. "So it does look as though she has a little bit of myopia. She could probably get by without glasses, but these things tend to get worse with age. If you don't do it now, you'll be doing it next year."

Cassie held her breath while her mother considered. Finally Mrs. Jones turned to her.

"What do you think, Cassie? Should we do glasses now or wait?"

"Now!" Cassie burst out. She hopped from the chair. "Can I go pick out my frames?"

Mrs. Jones gave a helpless shrug. "I guess so."

The doctor followed them out of the examining room. "These are the kids' frames," he said, leading them over to a wall with smaller, colorful frames.

"These are nice," her mom said, picking up a pair of burgundy wire ones.

Ew. No way. Cassie wrinkled her nose. She spotted a pair of thick, turquoise frames and pulled them loose.

She let out a gasp. They had sparkles and colored dots mixed inside the plastic, extending all the way through the arm that hooked over the ear.

"These, Mom! I love these!"

"Those?" Her mom arched an eyebrow.

"Oh, those are quite popular with the kids," the receptionist said with a chuckle. "All the bright colors."

"Yep." Cassie held them out. "Can I wear them home?"

"Oh, no, honey." The receptionist came around her desk and stood with Cassie and her mom. "Now that you've picked out your frames, we'll order them from the company. They'll put in your lenses so that when the glasses come, they're made for your eyes and your eyes only."

Cassie frowned. She'd envisioned walking out of here with her new glasses on, and showing up at school tomorrow all decked out. "How long's that going to take?"

"Oh, about two weeks." She looked down at Cassie through her own wire frames and smiled. "Not long. They'll be here before you know it."

Cassie nodded and put them back, trying to hide her disappointment. Two more weeks. Two whole weeks before anyone even knew she'd gotten glasses.

CHAPTER FOUR

Club Meeting

Thursday evening finally arrived. Cassie and Emily took the family phone into their room.

"I hope the battery doesn't die while we're using it," Cassie commented, hands on her hips. She surveyed everything they'd set up for their first Babysitters Club meeting. "People are probably going to be calling all evening."

"You girls have everything you need?" her mom

asked, poking her head in the room.

"Yep," Cassie and Emily chorused.

Cassie ticked the items off on her fingers. "We've got the phone. The appointment book. A pencil, of course. It's almost time!"

As if on cue, the doorbell rang. Emily bolted from the room, and Cassie ran after her.

"Hello!" a man's voice boomed from the doorway.

"Hey, Steve!" Mr. Jones said enthusiastically, grabbing his arm and pumping it. "So you're Danelle's father!" He looked at Cassie. "I work with him, Cassie."

"Wow," Cassie said. "That's cool." She grabbed Danelle's arm and hauled her into her room.

Danelle giggled. "Your dad's funny."

"Yeah," Cassie agreed.

Danelle took off her sweater and sat down on the bed. She looked around Cassie and Emily's room. "I like your decorations."

Cassie glanced around, too, wondering what Danelle liked. There was a poster of Dalmatians on the wall and a collection of American Girl dolls on the bed frame. But that was it. Maybe she liked the wallpaper? "Thanks." Emily nudged her, and she added, "This is my sister, Emily."

"Hi," Danelle said. "I've seen you around. Is Riley coming?"

"Um. . . ." Cassie checked her watch. Just a little after seven. "She said she was." She stared at the phone. "I could call her, I guess, but what if someone tries to call while I am?"

"You just click over to the other call," Danelle said. "You know how to do that, right?"

Actually, no. Cassie hardly ever used the phone. "Oh, right. I can do that." She grabbed her address book from under the bed, glad she'd written in Riley's phone number. She dialed the number.

"Hello?" Mrs. Isabel's voice answered.

"Hi, this is Cassie. Is Riley there?"

"Hi, Cassie. Sure, hang on one moment."

A second later, Riley got on. "Hello?" she said, not sounding very enthusiastic.

"Hey, we've started our club meeting. Aren't you coming?"

Silence followed on the other end. Finally Riley said, "I can't tonight."

There was no further explanation. Cassie rested her head against the wall. What could she say? She could guilt-trip her and make her feel bad for ditching. Or she could try to make her convince her parents. Neither would work, though. Riley wasn't coming. "Okay, well, we'll miss you," she said instead, and hung up. "She's not coming," she announced.

Danelle raised her eyebrows and settled back on the

bottom bunk. "Well, I guess that's not a big surprise, is it?"

Cassie wondered again what the deal was between Danelle and Riley. "Let's get started, then! I'm calling this meeting to order." She sat cross-legged on the floor, facing the other two girls. Opening one of her notebooks, she said, "Date. October 3. Members present: Emily Jones, Cassandra Jones, and Danelle Pierce." She tapped the pencil eraser against her lips. "Anything else I should write?"

"That we're awesome!" Danelle said, making a fist and thrusting it in the air.

Cassie put the minute book down and opened her appointment book. "Now we just wait for people to call."

The three of them stared at the phone. Cassie willed it to ring.

"We could play Uno while we wait," Emily said.

The phone began to jingle. Cassie had never thought of it that way before, but it wasn't really a ring. It was a melody. She dove for it, but Emily was faster.

"Did you need the Jones' residence or the Babysitters club?" she asked.

Cassie groaned. Claudia had her own phone line in the book, which meant no one had to guess if the caller wanted her or her family.

"Oh, you want to talk to him?" Emily's face fell. "Sure, I'll get him." She pulled the phone away and whispered, "It's for Daddy."

Cassie grabbed the phone and took it down the hall to the living room. "Daddy. Phone's for you." She handed it to him, but didn't let go. "Hurry! We're having our meeting right now!"

"I'll be quick," he said, locking eyes with her and nodding solemnly.

Emily had the Uno game out when Cassie returned

and was dealing out cards. Cassie couldn't think about the game. She sat on her hands, tapping the carpet with her toe. Someone could be trying to call right now. Would her dad click over? He knew how to do that, right?

Someone tapped on the door, and then her dad poked his arm in, phone extended in his hand. "Any luck yet?" he asked.

"Not yet," Cassie said, taking the phone. "Did anyone call while you were on it?"

"Nope. No one."

No one else called during the entire hour. They finished up their game of Uno, and then Danelle's dad was back to get her.

"I'm sure it was because it was our first night," Cassie said, trying to keep her spirits up. "Next Thursday will go better."

"I"m sure that's all it was," Mr. Pierce said. "Night,

51

Jim."

"Night, Steve!" Mr. Jones said, all big smiles.

Cassie rolled her eyes and went back to her room. What a bummer of a night.

♥

"How was your club meeting last night?" her mom asked her when she got off the bus Friday. "You went to bed so fast, I didn't get the chance to talk to you."

Cassie unloaded her backpack on the kitchen table. "It didn't go well," she said, zipping it shut. "Nobody called."

"Well, it was your first meeting," Mrs. Jones said. "I'm sure it will go better."

These were the same things Cassie had told herself the night before, but today she wasn't in the mood to be placated. "And what if it doesn't?" She crossed her arms over her chest and faced her mom. "If people don't call us to babysit, our club is pretty worthless."

"Didn't you have fun anyway?"

She considered the question and lifted one shoulder. "I guess." But that wasn't the point. It wasn't supposed to be a fun Uno club.

"I've got a babysitting job for you," Mrs. Jones said.

"You don't count," Cassie said in frustration. "I always babysit for you. You don't pay enough, anyway."

Her mom burst out laughing. "Well, let's think about this." She pulled out a chair and sat at the table. "Come, sit."

Cassie heaved a sigh and sat.

"What did you do to prepare for your babysitters club?"

"Well, I invited babysitters. We took notes, role, and waited. As soon as we get our first appointment, I want to make fun babysitting bags to take with us. I have some ideas for that."

Mrs. Jones nodded. "These are all great things, Cassie. How did you get the word out about your club?"

"Get the word out?" Cassie echoed.

"Yes. Who knew about your club? Who did you give your phone number to so they could call and hire you?"

"No one," Cassie said, feeling her heart sink like an anchor. Why hadn't she thought of that? No one would call her if they didn't even know.

"Well, that at least is something you can change," her mom said. "Let's make up some fliers tonight for your club, and tomorrow you can take them through the neighborhood and hand them out to everyone."

Cassie nodded, the anchor lifting from her heart and her spirit lightening. "Okay! That's a good plan."

Cassie's mom helped her design a simple black and white flier on the computer. They didn't have a copy machine, so Cassie counted up the houses in the neighborhood to see how many she needed to print.

"There's the Davidsons, the Maguires—but they only have a dog—"

"Take them one anyway," her mom said. "They might know someone with kids. Or maybe they have nieces and nephews."

Cassie nodded. "The Coys, the Webbs, the Thompsons, the Howards, the Rodriguezes, the Ruperts, the Lorries, and. . . ." That was it. Their rural community only had a small spattering of houses. And most of those didn't have small kids. "There's a few houses on the other street."

Her mom shook her head. "You're not allowed to walk down there. Give some fliers to Danelle and Riley, and tell them to hand them out to their neighbors."

Cassie thought of Riley's apartment complex and nodded, but she knew Danelle's neighbors were just as spread out as hers. "I'll take some to church, too."

"Good idea. Print off about forty, then. Ten for each of you and ten for church."

Forty sounded like a great number. She started the print job and waited for the pages to come out.

♥

Cassie woke up to the sounds of her younger brother and sister running through the house, laughing and yelling. She wasn't ready to get up yet. She didn't want to. She rolled over and squeezed her eyes shut, pretending like she hadn't woken. The bed felt so delicious and comfortable, and Saturday was the only day she got to sleep in.

Her eyes snapped open as she remembered the fliers she and her mom had made. Today was a special day. This was the day she would get her club going!

"Good morning. Glad to see you up before nine," her dad said when she came in for breakfast. He had his grubby clothes on, and Cassie tensed. She needed to hurry and lay out her plans for the day, or he'd have her out in the garden, picking up rocks.

"Good morning. I'm delivering fliers through the neighborhood to advertise my babysitting club," she said in a rush, pouring a bowl of cereal. She stuffed a spoonful in her mouth to keep from saying anything else.

"Oh. How very entrepreneurial of you."

Cassie squinted at him. She'd heard that word before, but she couldn't think of what it meant. "Which is?"

"Very businesslike. Very professional." He finished making himself a shake and left the room.

Cassie mapped out her plan. She'd start at the bottom of the hill and work her way back up. If she started at the top, by the time she finished she wouldn't want to climb back up.

She combed her hair nicely and put on a headband to

keep it out of her face. Then she added a gold chain with a medallion of a young girl and her favorite earrings, a pair of lime-green springs.

"Mom!" she called. "I'm going to hand out my fliers!"

"All right!" her mom called back from downstairs.

Cassie gripped the fliers in her hands and went outside. The crisp autumn air greeted her, but she knew by the time she reached the bottom of the hill, it would be warm. It was almost a full mile from her house to the end of the street.

Sure enough, when she reached the bottom twenty minutes later, she was not cold at all. She walked up to the Rupert's house and knocked on the door.

"Well, hello, Cassie!" Mrs. Rupert said, answering. "What are you doing down here?"

"My friends and I have started a babysitters club," Cassie said, reciting her rehearsed speech. "Here's a flier that tells you all about it. We'd love to babysit your children anytime you need us. Just call that number on the flier on Thursday evenings." She paused here in case Mrs. Rupert wanted to say something.

"Thank you, Cassie, what a lovely idea," Mrs. Rupert said.

"Thank you!" Cassie replied. She turned and trotted down the driveway, quite pleased with how that had gone.

Cassie continued her way up the hill. A lot of people weren't home, so she stuck fliers in their mailboxes. Everyone was very polite, smiling and thanking her, and Cassie felt optimistic that they'd start to get some business.

The last house was the Maguires. They were the ones that didn't have kids, but her mom thought she should go there anyway. Cassie started down their long, blacktop driveway, clutching her remaining fliers and humming to herself.

The driveway led into a four-door garage, while the house sat to the left of the driveway. Cassie turned toward the house when a low growling stopped her. She swiveled in the direction of the sound to see a large brown dog approaching her. He had his head low between his shoulders.

Another growl to her right made her gasp. She jumped around to see a second dog there. Her heart battered at her throat like a bird in a cage, seeking a way out. *Don't act afraid.* She'd heard that somewhere before, right? "Hello, doggies," she said. "Nice doggies." She held out a hand, noting how it shook.

The dog snarled and lunged at her, and she took a step backward. *Help*, she thought. She wanted to turn around and run, but she knew, just knew, that these dogs would chase her up the hill. She met one of the dog's eyes, trying to give it the impression that she couldn't be intimidated.

She thought she'd seen the Maguires pull into the driveway right before she got here. Maybe they would hear her. "Mr. Maguire!" she shouted.

Immediately both dogs launched into a chorus of barking and snarling. One skittered backwards on his feet, he was so wound up. The other dove at her, snapping and barking.

Cassie screamed. She couldn't help it; she was officially terrified. The dog stopped a few feet from her, but both of them continued the threatening barking. Cassie gave up on any semblance of calmness and screamed as loud as she could.

CHAPTER FIVE

New Dog

Cassie stared at the dogs, trying to keep both in her line of sight. They stared back at her, saliva dripping from their snarling mouths. What would her mom do when she didn't come back? Would the dogs tire of her before she got tired of standing here staring at them? Would someone come looking for her?

Her only hope was to attract the attention of whoever was inside. She screamed again, so loud her throat ached. Her ears rang, but the dogs barked harder, and she doubted anyone heard her. She put her hands over her ears, too frightened even to cry.

The front door opened, and Mr. Maguire stepped out. He was an older gentleman with a bald spot on the top of his head. He wore suspenders over a striped shirt. "What's all this ruckus, fellas?" he began, and then he spotted Cassie.

"Down, boys," he yelled, clapping his hands. "Back away!"

Obediently the dogs stopped. The stubby little tails dropped, and the dogs skulked back to the garage.

"What are you doing here?" Mr. Maguire said. "Are you hurt?"

Cassie shook her head, though her whole body trembled. "I was screaming."

He looked at her, his gray eyes apologetic. "I didn't hear you, hon. I came out to see why the dogs wouldn't stop barking. You shouldn't wander over to people's houses that you don't know."

Cassie couldn't agree more. She held out a flier, waited for him to take it. Then she walked back up his long driveway, hoping her shaky legs wouldn't give out on her.

♥

"I can't believe you were attacked by dogs," Danelle said, taking the fliers Cassie handed her at recess.

"Not attacked," Cassie corrected. "Just threatened." She looked at Riley and hesitated. "Do you want some?"

Riley shrugged. "I don't know if I'll be able to come."

"Well, take some anyway." Cassie put a few in her hands. "Hand them out to your neighbors. Maybe they need babysitters too."

"Yeah, okay."

"This is great." Danelle tucked her fliers into her

back pocket. "I'm sure we'll have more callers next time."

"Why couldn't you come last time, Riley?" Cassie ventured. She didn't want to cause an argument, but she felt like they deserved to know.

"No one wanted to drive me."

That made sense. Riley didn't have any control over that. "Well, maybe someone can drive you next time."

"Maybe."

♥

Cassie spooned some rice onto her plate and waited for the grilled chicken to make its way to her. "I gave Riley and Danelle fliers. I'm pretty sure we'll have plenty of people calling on Thursday."

"That's great, honey." Her mom met her dad's eyes across the table and smiled at him.

Cassie glanced at her dad, not sure if her parents were flirting with each other or laughing at her.

"Are you doing okay after those dogs attacked you?" Mr. Jones asked, accepting the bowl of rice from Emily.

Cassie scowled. "They didn't attack me. I was frightened, yeah, but I wasn't hurt."

"I just mean, will you be okay around other dogs?"

"Of course," she scoffed. "I'm not suddenly thinking every dog I see is going to hold me hostage in someone's driveway."

"I'd be scared," Annette said. "I'd never go near a dog again."

"You're afraid of everything," Scott said.

"No, just mean things," Annette protested.

"She's only four," Cassie said, shooting a glare at Scott. "She's allowed to be scared. Leave her alone."

The doorbell rang, and Scott and Annette pushed away from the table, already racing for the door.

"Who would come over now?" Cassie said, glancing at her mom. To her surprise, her mom's eyes were crinkled in a smile.

"Why don't you go see?" she replied.

Curious now, Cassie got up from the table.

"Hi, kids," a familiar voice was saying from the entryway. "Is your mom here?"

Cassie rounded the corner and saw Mrs. Isabel standing there. Riley stood behind her, holding Scaredy in her arms. Cassie cocked her head and frowned.

"Oh, hey," Riley said, spotting her. She gave a smile, but it trembled around the edges. "Here." She held out the dog.

"Hi, Karen," Mrs. Isabel said, her eyes looking over Cassie's shoulder. "I hope we're not late."

"Right on time," Mrs. Jones said, placing a hand on Cassie's arm. "Cassie, aren't you going to get your dog?"

Cassie whirled around, her eyes going wide. "My

dog?" she gasped.

"Unless you're afraid, of course," her mom teased.

Cassie faced Riley, unable to believe it.

"Here," Riley said again, shoving Scaredy into her arms.

Cassie let out a shriek of joy, and the dog cowered, his whole body trembling. His tail curled around his leg, and a pebble of poo hit the carpet. Cassie didn't care. She held him against her. "Mine? He's mine." She pressed her face to his and rubbed his nose.

"Yours," her mom confirmed.

Scott started up a chorus about how he wanted a dog, and Emily joined in, but Cassie paid them no mind. She thought of Riley and looked at her friend anxiously, worried she would be angry.

But she was smiling. "He'll be happy here. And I can come see him."

"Absolutely!" Cassie exclaimed. She reached over

and hugged Riley, her throat suddenly thick. "Thank you, thank you, thank you. Thank you so much."

♥

Cassie didn't know the first thing to do with a dog. It didn't take more than an hour to figure out that it was potty training. She took the dog for a walk, but he didn't poop. They came back in the house, and he found a cozy corner of the living room to relieve himself. The next hour she tried again, and still nothing. And the next hour.

"How often do I have to do this?" she asked her dad.

"Every hour," he replied. "It's the only way the dog will learn."

She got ready for bed and brought Scaredy into her room, where he crawled under her bed and trembled.

"He can't sleep with you," Mrs. Jones said, coming into the room. "We need to bathe him first and get him house broken. Tonight he'll sleep in the bathroom."

"In the bathroom!" Cassie gasped out. "He'll hate it there!"

"He'll get over it," her mom promised.

She and her mom laid down newspapers on the bathroom floor and gave him a bowl of water. Their other dog, Pioneer, kept poking his head inside to see what was going on. At least he was a friendly dog and didn't seem threatened by Scaredy.

Cassie hated closing the door on him, leaving him there, but she did. She lay in bed thinking about him, so glad he was hers and wondering how he was.

And then the whimpering started. It was so quiet, Cassie wasn't sure she'd really heard it. She held very still and strained her ears. There it came again. A quiet, mournful sound. It didn't get any louder, and she doubted anyone else could hear it. Cassie snuck out of bed and tiptoed to the bathroom. Pressing her ear against the door, she listened. Sure enough, the faint cry came from inside.

She opened the door and went in, turning on the light so she could see. Scaredy cowered by the toilet. The newspapers by the bathtub were peed on, but the rest of the bathroom was clean. Cassie got a towel from under the sink and put it on the floor. Then she turned off the light and lay down on top of it.

♥

Cassie woke up sometime during the night. She had no idea what time it was; the bathroom was pitch black. Her legs felt cold, but not her chest. Curled up beside her, little body lifting and lowering with each breath, was Scaredy. A happy feeling settled in her throat and filled her body. Cassie wrapped her arm around him and went back to sleep.

Or tried to. A moment later the bathroom door opened and shoved into her back.

"Ow," Cassie said.

The light turned on. Scaredy stood up and scurried behind the toilet. Emily stared down at her. "What are you doing in here?"

"Keeping the dog company." As if that weren't obvious. "He was crying."

"Well, the alarm went off. Better get ready for school."

"Did you wake Scott?"

"Not yet." Emily pulled the door closed, and Cassie assumed she'd gone to wake their brother.

She went behind the toilet and clicked her tongue, brushing her thumb and forefinger together, beckoning to Scaredy. He took two tiny steps toward her, and Cassie petted his little head.

"You'll be safe here," she told him. "And as soon as I get home, I'll come and see you."

The day dragged on at school. Riley asked how Scaredy was, but she lost interest about two minutes into Cassie's enthusiastic explanation about how last night had gone and what he was doing now. Cassie told Danelle instead, who thought it was cool that she had a new dog.

"What kind is he?" she asked.

"A beagle," Cassie replied, though she had no idea if that was true. It didn't matter to her. But she got the feeling it would matter to Danelle.

"Cool," she said. "Can't wait to see him on Thursday."

In Girls' Club after school, they started a cross-stitching project. It was fun, and Cassie enjoyed picking out the pattern and then choosing her thread. But her mind kept going back to the little dog waiting for her at home. When she saw her mom's blue van, she pushed her project back in the box and shouted a goodbye as she ran out the door.

"How is he?" she asked, shutting the car door and

turning to her mother.

"Ask Annette," her mom replied. "She's been playing with him all day."

A stab of envy pierced Cassie's heart. She knew she should feel grateful; she should thank Annette, and be glad that Scaredy wasn't home alone and sad all day. But really, she was jealous. Would the dog like Annette more now? She gave her little sister a weak smile. "Thanks for doing that. How is he?"

"Great!" Annette said cheerfully, kicking her legs in her booster chair.

As soon as Mrs. Jones parked the blue van in the driveway, Cassie hopped out of the car. She ran into the house and made a bee-line for the hall bathroom. Scaredy lifted his head from his front paws and blinked at her when she came in. He didn't run and hide, and Cassie's heart warmed.

"Hello," she cooed, setting her backpack on the sink.

"How are you?" She got out her homework assignment and sat down on the toilet with it. Today she'd get her work done in here, with her dog.

CHAPTER SIX

Multiplication

"Today we're going to do a multiplication test," Ms. Dawson said, setting a timer on her desk. "For those of you who haven't done this before, I'll hand out the test face down. You leave it that way until I say go. It has one hundred problems on it, and you'll have one minute. When the minute is up, mark the spot you got to and then finish up the test."

Cassie sat up straighter, clasping her hands together

76

on her desk. She shoved thoughts of Scaredy from her head and focused on the task at hand. Her last school had put a huge emphasis on the times tables. She'd memorized almost all of the single digit multiplication, and was quite certain she could finish this test in one minute.

Ms. Dawson placed a test face-down on her desk, and Cassie put her finger on the edge of it, pencil ready. Her heart did a drum roll in anticipation.

"All right," Ms. Dawson said, returning to her desk. She picked up the little white timer and spun the dial. "Ready, set, go."

Cassie flipped her paper over and started writing down the answers. Each problem drew the answer from her brain as if it were a magnet. For the past three years her teachers had drilled these in, putting a huge focus on sight recognition. It was paying off now. Forty-nine, eighty-one, sixteen. Her pencil couldn't move as fast as her brain did.

She was almost there. She didn't dare look at the timer as she started on the last row of problems. Sixty-four, nine—

"Time!" Ms. Dawson called. "Everyone put a line on your paper so I know how far you got. And then do the rest."

Cassie exhaled as her heart rate slowly descended, disappointment replacing her excitement. She drew a line after problem number ninety-four. She still had six more. She finished them up, turned her paper over, and put her pencil on top. She glanced around at her classmates, still working hard on their problems. No one else had finished.

"Are you done?" Emmett whispered beside her.

"I think so," Cassie said, not wanting to sound too confident lest he think she was boasting.

"Already?" Sara Berry said. Cassie could see from

where her pencil hovered that Sara had two more rows to go.

Cassie nodded. She reached into her desk and pulled out *The Babysitters Club* book she was reading.

"Anyone still working?" Ms. Dawson asked. When nobody raised their hand, she smiled and walked to the front of the room with her answer key in hand. "All right, let's check. Whoever didn't miss any will get a prize."

Cassie looked at the six she hadn't finished in time. She knew she wouldn't get a prize.

Ms. Dawson began calling out the answers. Cassie felt a sense of pride as she checked off each one. So far she hadn't missed any.

"Yes!" Brenna Atkins whispered loudly.

Nobody paid her any mind. Brenna often drew attention to herself during class.

Ms. Dawson called out the next answer.

"Yay!" Brenna squealed.

The teacher called out another.

"Yes!" Brenna said, not even whispering. She pumped her fist.

Cassie tried not to roll her eyes. Apparently they were going to get a to-the-second update on Brenna's score.

Ms. Dawson kept going, and Brenna kept cheering for herself all the way to the end. Cassie did her best to tune her out. In spite of not finishing on time, she was quite pleased that she hadn't missed any.

"Did anyone get a perfect score?" Ms. Dawson asked.

"Me! Me!" Brenna's hand shot up so fast and wiggled so hard that it lifted her from her chair.

Cassie frowned, her stomach giving a little jolt of displeasure. She knew Brenna hadn't finished before the timer went off. She'd watched her finish up her test long after Cassie had turned hers over. But she kept her mouth shut. It was none of her business if Brenna wanted to cheat and lie. She swallowed hard.

"Let's see, then." Ms. Dawson took Brenna's paper and started going over it. "Oops, nope, Brenna, you missed one." She circled a problem with her red pencil and handed it back. "Sorry."

Brenna heaved a sigh and sank back in her chair.

"Anyone else not miss any?" Ms. Dawson's eyes surveyed the room.

"How many did you miss, Cassie?" Sara asked.

Emmett peered over his desk at Cassie's paper. "You didn't miss any. Raise your hand."

"I finished after the timer went off," Cassie said.

"You didn't miss any!" Sara hissed, grabbing Cassie's paper.

"But I didn't finish!" Cassie protested, trying to retrieve her test from Sara.

"Ms. Dawson, Cassie didn't miss any," Sara said

loudly, holding up the paper.

"I didn't finish before the timer went off," Cassie said, hating that she had to rat herself out.

"That doesn't matter," Ms. Dawson said, approaching their desks. "Did you miss any?"

Cassie shook her head.

Ms. Dawson took the paper and stood there as she went over it. Then she handed it back. "Congratulations, Cassandra. You didn't miss any." She returned to the front and faced the class. "Not only did she not miss any, but Cassie only had six left when the timer went off. Bravo, Cassandra. You did fantastic."

Cassie's face warmed under the praise, but her heart swelled with pride. Her classmates congratulated her. Cassie murmured her thanks, keeping her eyes lowered. But inside she glowed, pleased that she excelled at something, at least.

CHAPTER SEVEN

End of a Club

Cassie ran home from the bus stop and headed straight for the bathroom. Her mom stopped her.

"You don't have time to play with the dog right now. We have somewhere to go."

Cassie paused with her hand on the doorknob. "Where are we going?"

"To the eye doctor." A smile quirked around the edges of her mother's mouth. "Your glasses are here."

Cassie let out a squeal of delight. "Let me just say hi to him real quick."

Twenty minutes later they arrived at the doctor's office in downtown Fayetteville. Cassie jumped around from foot to foot while her mother spoke to the receptionist.

"We're here to pick up some glasses. Cassandra Jones."

"Oh, of course." The woman smile and disappeared into a room in the back. She returned with a white case and pair of bright turquoise glasses in her hands. "This look familiar?"

Cassie squinted at them. It had been so long, she couldn't be sure.

"Let's look in the mirror." She directed Cassie to the mirror next to the kids' glasses and placed them on Cassie's face. "How do those look?"

Everything sharpened to the point of being slightly

too close. She tilted her head. The large round frames made her eyes seem smaller behind the lenses. She pulled them off and examined them. Sure enough, they had the colored, floating polka dots inside the plastic. She put them back on and smiled at her reflection. She looked different.

"What do you think, Mom?" she asked, meeting her mom's eyes in the mirror.

"They look great, Cassie. They're the ones you picked out, right?"

"Right." Cassie nodded, examining herself again. She gave a nod. "Yeah. I like them." It would take some getting used to, though, especially when her vision changed at the corners of her eyes.

❤

She almost forgot to put her glasses on in the mad rush to get to the bus the next morning, but at the last minute remembered. She slid them on, a bit

85

apprehensive. What would her classmates think? She trapped her long dark hair behind a headband and gave her reflection a cursory glance. She looked tired, but she'd spent the night in the bathroom again, so that wasn't too surprising.

She climbed on the bus and looked for Betsy, who got on before her. She spotted her hanging over the back of her seat, poking Chad Cameron with her pencil. Cassie plopped down next to her, and Betsy turned around.

"Hey!" she exclaimed. "You got glasses!"

"Yep." Cassie beamed, excited that she'd noticed right away.

"How fun! Do you like them?"

"Love them," she said, sliding her backpack around to her chest. "Do you?"

"They look great! Everyone's going to love them."

Cassie straightened up in her seat, feeling more confident already.

♥

"I love your glasses," Danelle said at recess. She and Riley and Cassie sat under one of the trees, picking dandelions and looking for four-leaf clovers.

"Thanks," Cassie said. "You're coming over tonight, right?"

"Yep. My dad's bringing me."

"And you?" Cassie looked at Riley.

"Yeah," she said, "I think so."

"Did you guys hand out your fliers?"

"I did," Danelle said. "My mom took them to work and handed them out, also."

Riley didn't answer, and Cassie didn't press her. That meant she hadn't.

Ms. Dawson blew her whistle, and the three girls stood up.

"I'll see you tonight!" Cassie said.

♥

Danelle was the first to arrive, at about five to seven. Outside, the night air had turned nippy, so Cassie took her jacket and hung it up. Mr. Pierce went into the living room to talk to Mr. Jones.

"Riley's not here yet," Cassie said. "Come see my new dog."

Scaredy had graduated from the bathroom and moved to her room. She'd walked him outside earlier and considered him successfully house trained. He lifted his head from Cassie's blanket and batted his little tail against the ground, a soft *thump thump thump.*

"Oh, he's cute!" Danelle said, crouching down in front of him. He backed his head up but didn't stand.

"Yeah, he used to be so scared of us." Cassie sat next to him and patted his head. "I think he likes us now." As if on cue, he got up and crawled into her lap.

Emily came in with a bag of chips and a plate of cut fruit. "Snacks! It's seven."

"Great." Cassie opened up the notebook and took attendance. "Riley's not here," she stated.

"And she's probably not coming," Danelle added.

Probably. Cassie decided not to comment on that. "Well, it's time! Let's see who calls today!"

They waited wordlessly for the first five minutes. Cassie got up and got everyone water during the five after that. Emily offered to braid Danelle's hair, which annoyed Cassie, but Danelle said yes, so there wasn't anything she could do about it.

A knock sounded on the door, and then Mr. Jones poked his head in. "Anyone call yet?"

"Not yet," Cassie said, mustering a smile. "But I'm sure they will soon!"

"I'm sure," he replied. He closed the door.

The silence that followed felt heavy with expectation. Cassie studied her nails to avoid making eye contact with anyone else.

"What happens if no one calls?" Emily ventured.

Cassie didn't answer. She didn't know what to say.

"Someone will call eventually," Danelle said.

"But how long do we wait?" Emily pressed. "Do we keep meeting every Thursday, hoping that someone calls?"

Cassie bristled, annoyed with her little sister. "First off, Emily, you're only here because Mom said I had to include you. You're nine years old. No one's going to hire you to babysit."

Emily's brown eyes filled with tears. "Well, you're only ten!" she sputtered, and ran from the room.

"But I'm almost eleven!" Cassie shouted after her.

"Ten is a bit young," Danelle said. "I won't be eleven until next summer. Maybe we should try again in a year."

Cassie hunched her shoulders, feeling her grand idea deflating like a balloon with a hole in it. She knew in her gut that if they didn't make it work this time, they wouldn't try again. "I've been babysitting since I was nine."

Danelle shrugged. "Sure, but nobody else knows that."

Her eyes stung and she sniffled, trying to hold back the emotions. One tear snuck over the side, and she wiped it away. "So we should quit?"

"Maybe just for now," Danelle said. Her eyebrows lifted in a gesture of sympathy. "But we can try again when we're older."

"Yeah. Okay." Cassie put on a stiff smile. She knew this was the end. She tried to think of something more to say, something that might make Danelle want to come back every Thursday, but words failed her.

Danelle stood up. "Well, I guess I'll get my jacket. Thanks for trying this, anyway. It was fun."

Cassie folded her arms and nodded, not believing for

one second that Danelle had enjoyed these meetings. Boring and unproductive. Cassie felt like a total failure.

Mr. Jones came and put his arm around her shoulders as Danelle and her dad left. "So that's the end of it?"

A tear rolled down her cheek and she sniffed. "I guess."

He gave her a squeeze. "It was a good effort, Cassie. I'm excited for what you'll do in your future."

Not Cassie. She didn't even want to think about tomorrow.

"Cheer up, sweetheart." He nuzzled her hair and winked at her. "Your mom and I have a surprise for you guys."

"Really?" Her curiosity piqued, managing to dull some of her disappointment. Who didn't love a good surprise? "What is it?"

"We'll tell you at dinner tomorrow. Now come on. Let's go on out."

Available now!

Walker Wildcats Year 1

Episode 3: Road Trip

The first day of driving was uneventful and dull. Cassie started out strong doing her homework, but after about half an hour, she tired of it.

They crossed over into Tennessee and then Mississippi. Cassie fanned herself, noting that it was warming up in the car. "Daddy," she said, "it's getting hot back here."

"Turn the AC on, Jim," Mrs. Jones said.

"You do it," he replied. "I'm driving."

A moment later the cooler air began to kick out of the vents above Cassie's seat. "Must be nice weather outside," she said.

"Must be," Emily agreed. "I see the sun shining."

They listened to an audio book and endured Scott's constant nagging before finally reaching a hotel around ten at night.

Nobody was excited the next morning as Mr. Jones marched them into the car around six a.m. "Just eleven more hours," her mom said as everyone got seated. As if that was supposed to be reassuring.

Cassie ate her morning pop tart and went back to sleep. When she woke up, two hours had passed. She immersed herself in her stencils, and then started reading her second book. When she finished it, she sighed and tossed it on the seat beside her. Nothing was fun right now. "What's that smell?" she asked. At first she had thought it was someone's barbecue, but as it got stronger, it just smelled like something burning.

"Jim, pull over," her mom said, placing a hand on his arm and pointing out the window. Little puffs of smoke billowed up from the hood. Her dad grumbled something and Cassie sat up straighter, trying to see over her siblings' heads in the middle row.

"Is the car broken?" Emily asked.

"Let's hope not," Cassie said, consulting the watch on her wrist. They'd only been driving five hours. They were nowhere near their final destination.

Mr. Jones got out of the car and propped the hood up. Cassie undid her seatbelt, and her mom whipped around.

"Do not get out of your seat!" she ordered.

Cassie made a face and redid her seatbelt. A few minutes later, her dad got back in.

"I think it's overheating," he said. "I need to get it to a mechanic to look at."

Her mom looked around, and Cassie did too. They were on a highway somewhere in Georgia, with nothing around except thick trees, the colorful leaves still making their lazy descent from the upper branches to the ground. There weren't even any road signs or other cars driving around.

"Well, I guess we better pray it makes it to the next exit," Mrs. Jones sighed.

The next exit sign appeared ten minutes later, along with the words "No Services" written across the bottom. Mr. Jones put his blinker on, the steady *click click click* reaching all the way to the back of the car.

"Don't take that exit!" her mom snapped. "There's no services! We'll just waste our time driving around!"

He took of the blinker.

Five minutes later another sign appeared, this time with a few unrecognizable restaurants and gas stations listed.

"It's not really smoking anymore," Mr. Jones said. "Maybe it was just a piece of leaf or something that caught fire and had to burn off."

"If you think so," Mrs. Jones said.

"Yeah, I think we're good."

Cassie relaxed and pulled out another one of her

books. She knew she should work on her homework, but that wasn't nearly as interesting as reading. "Crisis averted," she told Emily. "The car's fine."

"Are we there yet?" Scott asked from the middle row.

"I'm hungry!" Annette announced for the hundredth time.

"Cassie, snacks," her mom said.

Cassie leaned over and opened the big green cooler between the two rows. "Grapes, anyone?"

As she handed out the green globes, she thought she smelled smoke again. She sniffed the air. "What's that smell?"

"Jim!" her mom exclaimed.

The tires squealed as the van veered to the right. Cassie grabbed onto Annette's chair as the car came to a screeching halt.

The adventure continues with Cassandra Jones in sixth grade! *Walker Wildcats Year 2* available now!

About the Author

Tamara Hart Heiner is a mom, wife, baker, editor, and author. She currently lives in Arkansas with her husband, four children, a cat, a guinea pig, and several fish. She would love to add a macaw and a sugar glider to the family. She's the author of several young adult suspense series as well as a nonfiction book about the Joplin Tornado, *Tornado Warning*.

Connect with Tamara online!
Facebook: *https://www.facebook.com/author.tamara.heiner*
website: *http://www.tamarahartheiner.com*

Thank you for reading!